Chuckie and the Lima Beans

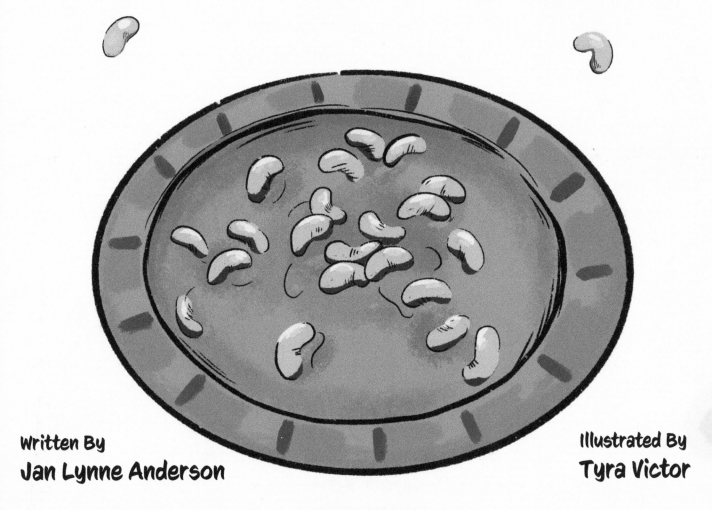

Written By
Jan Lynne Anderson

Illustrated By
Tyra Victor

Crosspointe Press
Cincinnati, Ohio

To: Charles A. Anderson---the original Chuckie
My thanks and gratitude for your endless love and support.

Written for Ruff Tuff Ronan, Sweet Baby Lylah,
Abigail the Builder and Adventure Girl Lindsay.
JLA

Library of Congress Control Number 2021904198

ISBN 978-1-7367354-3-5 (Hardback edition)

ISBN: 978-1-7367354-0-4 (Paperback Edition)

ISBN: 978-1-7367354-1-1 (eBook Edition)

Grandma's pot roast had been stringy and just a little bit hard to chew, but the brown gravy made it worth the effort.

And Grandma knew little pats of melty butter on the top of her creamy mashed potatoes were how Chuckie liked them.

But lima beans?

Even Grandma couldn't make lima beans taste good. Lima beans would lay like hard little nuggets in his mouth. Nasty tasting nuggets.

No, he wouldn't, he couldn't eat those lima beans.

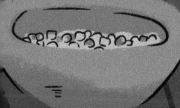

Chuckie's mother bobbed her head up and down, "Yes, eat your lima beans. Grandma made banana pudding for dessert. You want some banana pudding, don't you, Chuckie?"

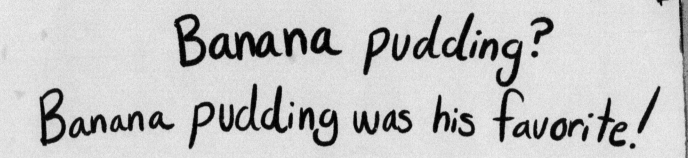

Banana pudding?
Banana pudding was his favorite!

Grandma probably had some of those yummy vanilla wafers to go on the side of the pudding, too. Of course, he wanted banana pudding! But first he would have to eat those nasty lima beans...

or would he?

Chuckie waited.
Sunday dinners at Grandma's
house were always lively.

Pretty soon the adults were busy talking and laughing. They weren't paying any attention to Chuckie.

Slowly, very slowly, his hand crept over to the pile of lima beans. Scooping them up, he swept them off his plate and down to his pants pocket. Gently, so as not to squash them, (as if you could squash the nasty little lumps),

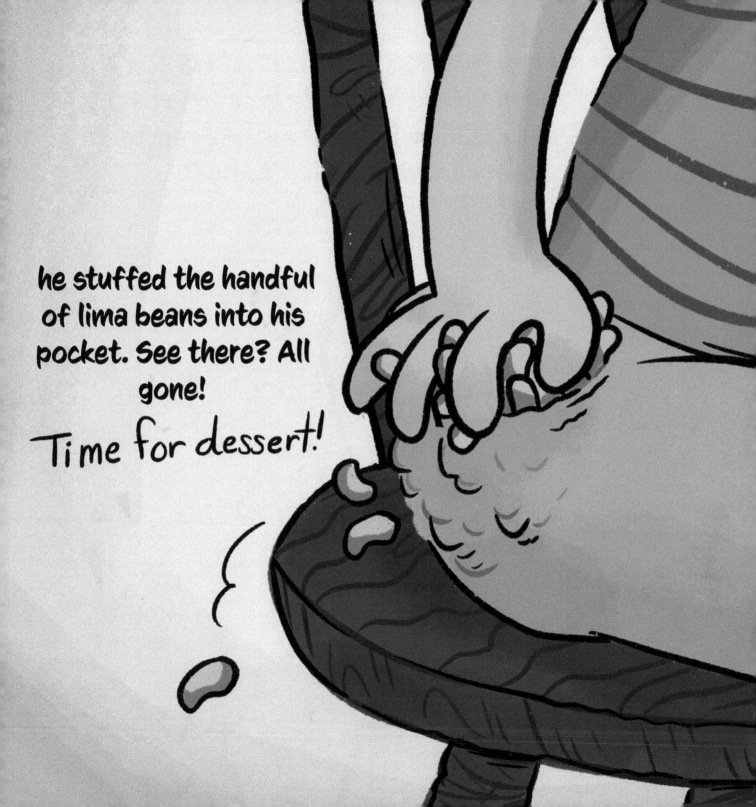

he stuffed the handful of lima beans into his pocket. See there? All gone!

Time for dessert!

Chuckie's father glanced over at his son's plate. "Why, Chuckie, you ate your lima beans. I guess you really wanted some of Grandma's banana pudding, didn't you?"

Chuckie nodded and gobbled up his helping of banana pudding. And yes, Grandma had remembered to put three vanilla wafers in his dish.

After dinner, Mother, Father and Chuckie visited with Grandma in the living room. Chuckie lay down on the floor and fell fast asleep watching TV. When it was time to go home, Father bent down to pick Chuckie up and carry him to the car.

As Father straightened up,
he heard "PlOP PlOP PlOP."
Looking down, he saw lima beans on the carpet.
Why on earth would lima beans be on the living
room carpet?

Then he heard "PlOP PlOP PlOP."
Father could see lima beans falling one by one
out of Chuckie's pocket. Father didn't
say anything, but he was angry.

PLOP

PLOP

PlOP

"You didn't eat your lima beans? Shame on you. You can't sleep here with us. Go sleep with the chickens," Big Dog growled.

Chuckie bumbled his way over to the pigpen. Butterball Pig looked up as Chuckie unfastened the gate.

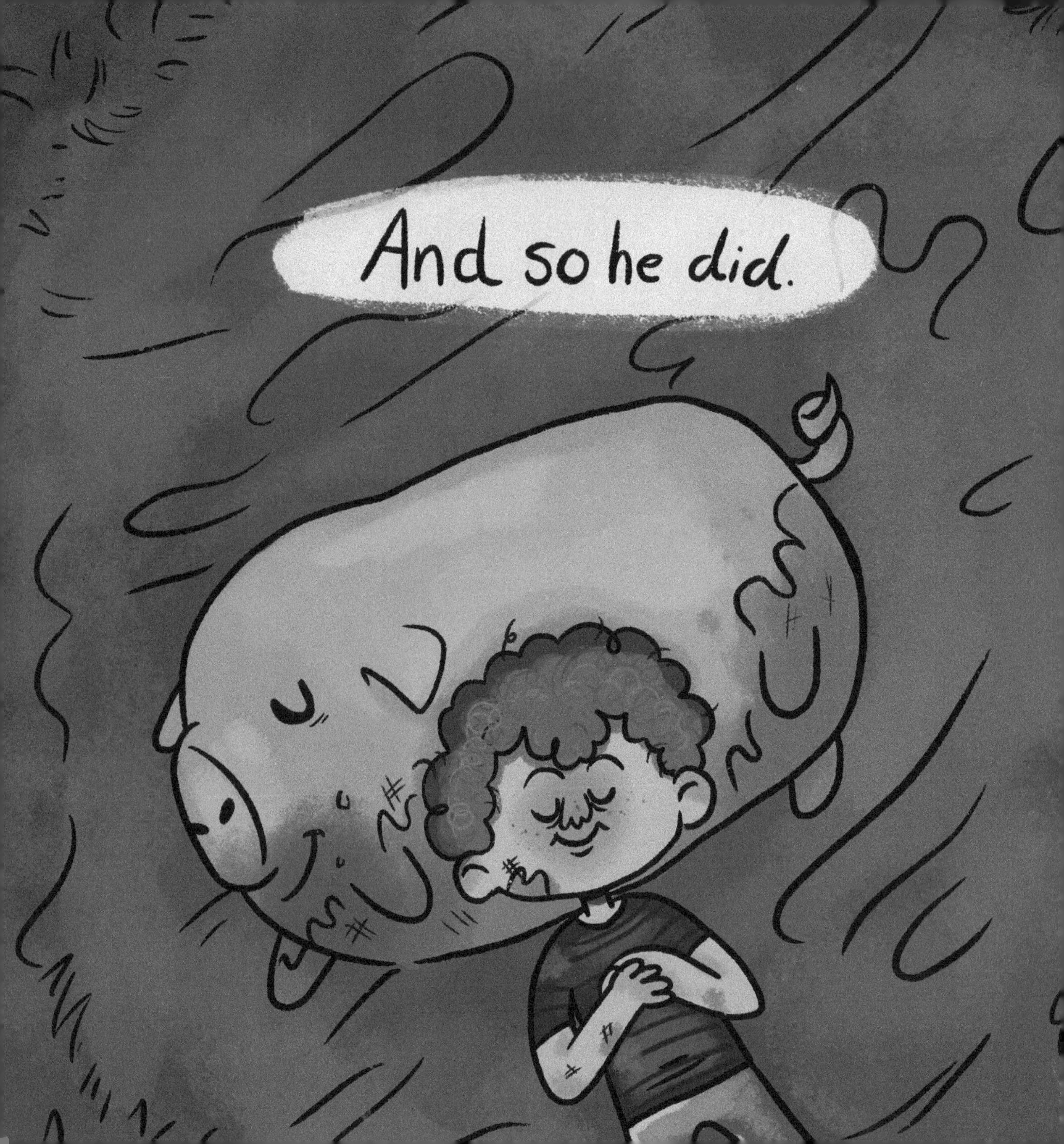
And so he did.

Part of this story is true, and part of it is not. Where do YOU think the truth ends and the tall tale begins?

9 781736 735404